Note to parents, carers and teachers

Read it yourself is a series of modern stories, favourite characters, traditional tales and first reference books written in a simple way for children who are learning to read. The books can be read independently or as part of a guided reading session.

Each book is carefully structured to include many high-frequency words vital for first reading. The sentences on each page are supported closely by pictures to help with understanding, and to offer lively details to talk about.

The books are graded into four levels that progressively introduce wider vocabulary and longer text as a reader's ability and confidence grows.

Ideas for use

- Begin by looking through the book and talking about the pictures. Has your child heard this story or looked at this subject before?

- Help your child with any words he does not know, either by helping him to sound them out or supplying them yourself.

- Developing readers can be concentrating so hard on the words that they sometimes don't fully grasp the meaning of what they're reading. Answering the quiz questions at the end of the book will help with understanding.

For more information and advice on Read it yourself and book banding, visit **www.ladybird.com/readityourself**

Book Band 5

Level 1 is ideal for children who have received some initial reading instruction. Stories are told, or subjects are presented very simply, using a small number of frequently repeated words.

Special features:

Opening pages introduce key subject words

Lots of pets

fish

hamster

guinea pig

dog

cat

rabbit

8

9

Careful match between text and pictures

Hamsters

Hamsters like to play.

They like to sleep a lot, like cats.

My hamster lives in here.

Large, clear labels and captions

hamster

18

Would you like a pet hamster?

19

Educational Consultant: Geraldine Taylor
Book Banding Consultant: Kate Ruttle
Subject Consultant: Dr Kim Dennis-Bryan

LADYBIRD BOOKS

UK | USA | Canada | Ireland | Australia
India | New Zealand | South Africa

Ladybird Books is part of the Penguin Random House group of companies
whose addresses can be found at global.penguinrandomhouse.com.

www.penguin.co.uk   www.puffin.co.uk   www.ladybird.co.uk

Penguin
Random House
UK

First published 2016
This edition 2019
002

Copyright © Ladybird Books Ltd, 2016

Printed in China

A CIP catalogue record for this book is available from the British Library

ISBN: 978-0-241-40540-6

All correspondence to:
Ladybird Books
Penguin Random House Children's
One Embassy Gardens, 8 Viaduct Gardens, London SW11 7BW

Favourite Pets

Written by Catherine Baker
Illustrated by Mark Ruffle

Contents

Lots of pets

fish

hamster

guinea pig

dog

cat

rabbit

Dogs

A dog can be a good pet.

Dogs are lots of fun!

11

Would you like a dog?

Dogs like to play and jump, and they eat a lot.

Dogs like to eat.

Cats

Cats can be good pets as well.

cat —

15

Would you like a cat?

Cats love to jump and play.

My cat loves to play. I can play with her.

They like to sleep a lot,
as well.

My cat likes
to sleep here.

Hamsters

Hamsters like to play.

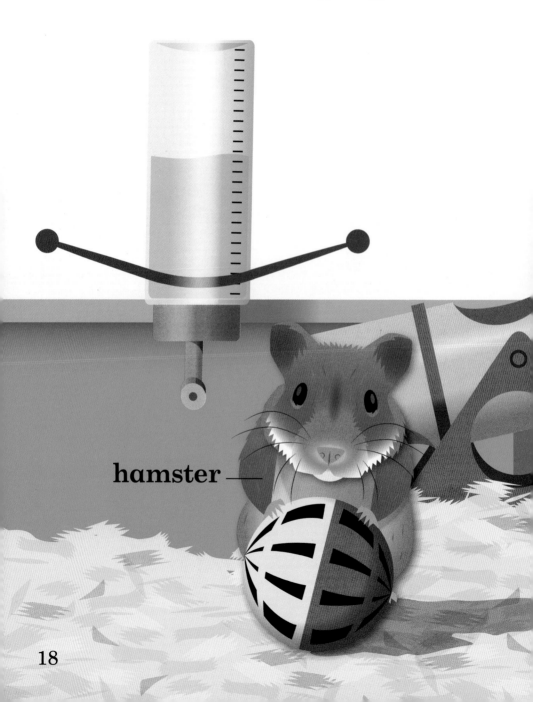

hamster ——

They like to sleep a lot,
like cats.

My hamster
lives in here.

Would you like a pet hamster?

Fish

Fish are fun to watch
and look after.

21

Rabbits

Rabbits love to play,
jump and eat.

rabbit

Would you like a pet rabbit?

Guinea pigs

Guinea pigs like to
live with a friend.

Guinea pigs love to play.

The guinea pigs love to play in here.

Vets and pets

The vet can help look after our pets.

The vet makes them well.

We love the vet!

Picture glossary

 cat

 dog

 eat

 fish

 guinea pig

 hamster

 jump

 rabbit

 sleep

 vet

Index

Favourite Pets quiz

**What have you learnt about pets?
Answer these questions and find out!**

- Which pets like to eat a lot?

- Which pets like to sleep a lot?

- Which pets like to live with a friend?

- Who makes pets well?

www.ladybird.com